THE FINAL SECRET OF Adolf Hitler

THE FINAL SECRET OF
Adolf Hitler

HUMANOIDS

WRITER
MATHIEU MARIOLLE

ARTIST
FABIO PIACENTINI

COLORIST
MASSIMO TRAVAGLINI

•

TRANSLATOR
MONTANA KANE

ENGLISH-LANGUAGE EDITION EDITOR
JONATHAN STEVENSON

ORIGINAL EDITION EDITORS
CAMILLE THÉLOT-VERNOUX & BRUNO LECIGNE

DESIGNER
SANDY TANAKA

SENIOR ART DIRECTOR
JERRY FRISSEN

PUBLISHER
MARK WAID

Rights and Licensing - licensing@humanoids.com
Press and Social Media - pr@humanoids.com

THE FINAL SECRET OF ADOLPH HITLER. First Printing.
This book is a publication of Humanoids, Inc. 8033 Sunset Blvd. #628, Los Angeles, CA 90046.

Library of Congress Control Number: 2021951710

HAMBURG. DECEMBER 1944.
SNOW'S GRAY IN GERMANY?
THAT'S NOT SNOW, IT'S ASH. THE AIR'S BEEN FULL OF IT SINCE THE AIR RAIDS STARTED LAST YEAR.

EITHER PIPE DOWN OR SPEAK GERMAN, BEFORE SOMEONE HEARS YOU.

Captain Duke Collins-- 5th Ranger Battalion-- U.S. Army.
WE'RE HERE.

WE'RE NOT GOING IN THE MAIN ENTRANCE, CAPTAIN?
NOT AFTER WHAT HAPPENED IN COLOGNE.

IF WE HAVE TO ENGAGE, I'D RATHER IT BE *AFTER* THE EXPLOSIVES ARE IN PLACE.
ALL CLEAR... WILSON, ADAMS, COME WITH ME...
MILLER, FITZGERALD, YOU TAKE THE OTHER SIDE OF THE PLANT.

WATCH OUT...

HIDE THE BODY AND CATCH UP WITH US.
WE GOTTA HURRY. I WANT THIS DONE BEFORE THE WORKERS GET HERE.
DON'T WANNA HAVE TO FIGHT OUR WAY OUT, CAP?
THE WORKERS HERE ARE PRISONERS, AND I'M SICK OF SACRIFICING INNOCENT LIVES.
WAS MACHEN SIE HIER?*
*WHAT ARE YOU DOING HERE?

LET'S GET OUTTA HERE!

EINDRINGEN!*
*INTRUDERS!

COULDN'T RESIST A LITTLE ACTION, HUH, CAPTAIN?

I KNOW HOW YOU GET BORED WITHOUT ANY SNAFUS!

MOVE IT, GUYS! SHE'S GONNA BLOW!
FLOOR IT, JONES!

WELL, THAT'S ONE STEP CLOSER TO THE END OF THIS FUCKING WAR.
I DOUBT IT... THE NAZIS ARE FANATICAL. THEY'LL *NEVER* SURRENDER.

KIEL U-BOAT BUNKER.
5 DECEMBER 1944.

WE'RE ALMOST DONE LOADING, COMMANDER.

HAVE THE BALLASTS AND THE SEALS ON THE SNORKEL CHECKED AGAIN.
KORVETTEN KAPITÄN RALF REIMAR WOLFRAM-- UNTERSEEBOOT-864

YOU'VE BEEN DOUBLE-CHECKING EVERYTHING FOR DAYS, WOLFRAM. IT'S TIME TO GO!
HAUPSTSTURMFÜHRER HANS KEMMLING-- WAFFEN-SS

I'M ONLY TRYING TO ENSURE NOTHING PREVENTS ME FROM COMPLETING MY MISSION.
OUR MISSION.

DON'T TAKE THAT TONE WITH ME.
IF IT WERE MY DECISION, YOU WOULDN'T BE A PART OF THIS MISSION AT ALL! I DON'T KNOW WHY THEY'VE GIVEN ME A *CHILD* FOR SUCH AN IMPORTANT JOB.
THE VETERANS LOYAL TO THE PARTY ARE ALL DEAD ALREADY.

WE'LL LEAVE AS SOON AS YOUR MEN ARE DONE LOADING.

AND YOU ARE *NOT* TO GIVE THEM OUR FINAL DESTINATION. IS THAT CLEAR?

IT'S TIME.
YES.

I HOPE YOU'RE GRATEFUL FOR THIS, WOLFRAM.
YOU'RE IN COMMAND OF THE BIGGEST SUB IN THE FLEET... AND OPERATION CAESAR IS GOING TO CHANGE THE COURSE OF THE WAR!

YES...

LET'S JUST HOPE IT ALL GOES TO PLAN...

THE CREW AWAIT YOUR ORDERS, CAPTAIN.
TAKE US DOWN TO 120 METERS.

FULL STEAM AHEAD!

OKAY, LET'S GO! WE HAVE OUR ORDERS!

BOW DOWN, STERN UP TEN.

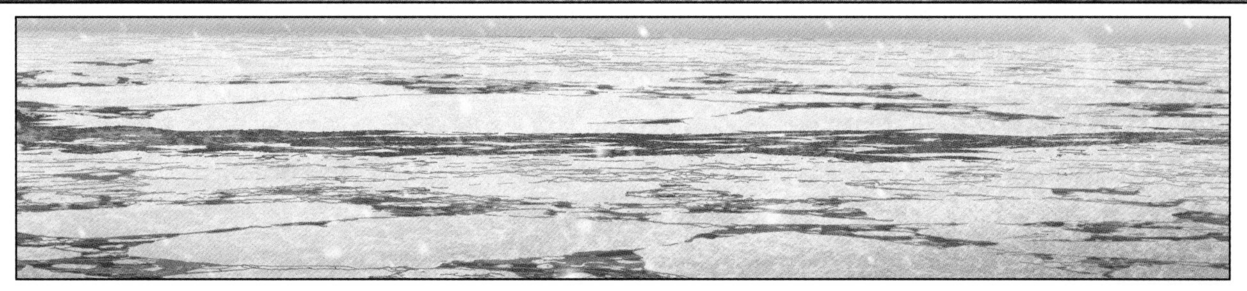

STILL NOTHING ON THE RADIO?

MILLER'S GLUED TO HIS SET. HE'LL TELL US AS SOON AS HE HEARS SOMETHING.

STILL STARING AT THOSE DAMN MAPS?
THE ONLY THING I CAN TRUST IN THIS WAR...

LOOK--OUR SIDE'S BREACHED THE SIEGFRIED LINE. THE RUSSIANS JUST CROSSED THE DANUBE.
WHOEVER REACHES BERLIN FIRST GETS TO END THIS WAR...*AND* GETS A HEAD START ON WHATEVER COMES NEXT.

WHAT'S THAT?
A SOUVENIR FROM HAMBURG.

THE AIR FORCE GUYS CALL THEM "WINDOWS." IT WAS THEIR MIRACLE WEAPON LAST YEAR.

"THEY'D DROP THOUSANDS OF THESE METALLIC FILAMENTS BEFORE EVERY AIR RAID.
"THEY'RE GREAT FOR MESSING WITH THE RADARS.

"THEY COULD GET IN, DROP THEIR PAYLOADS, AND GET OUT BEFORE ANYONE KNEW THEY WERE THERE.
"THEY FLATTENED WHOLE CITIES... ALL FOR THE GREATER GOOD..."

ARE YOU TRYING TO TELL ME SOMETHING, WILSON? THAT THERE'LL ALWAYS BE COLLATERAL DAMAGE?
NO, JUST THAT THE PENCIL-PUSHERS IN LONDON PROBABLY THINK IT'S HARDER TO DESTROY FACTORIES THAN THE PEOPLE WORKING IN THEM.
AND THAT I'D RATHER BE WITH YOU IN THE FIELD THAN BEHIND A DESK ANY DAY.

THE ORDERS HAVE COME IN, CAPTAIN.

IS THIS SOME KIND OF JOKE? THEY'RE SENDING US TO *NORWAY?!*

THE DESK JOCKEYS THINK WE'VE GOT IT TOO EASY HERE?
THEY WANT US TO GO HELP A RESISTANCE NETWORK THERE.
WHY NOT LET US KEEP RUNNING OPS IN GERMANY? I THOUGHT THE GOAL WAS TO GET TO BERLIN BEFORE THE RUSSIANS.

THE DAY THE TOP BRASS STARTS MAKING ANY SENSE, WE'LL BE WALKING ON THE MOON.
WHAT DO YOU THINK, MILLER?
ORDERS ARE ORDERS, CAPTAIN.

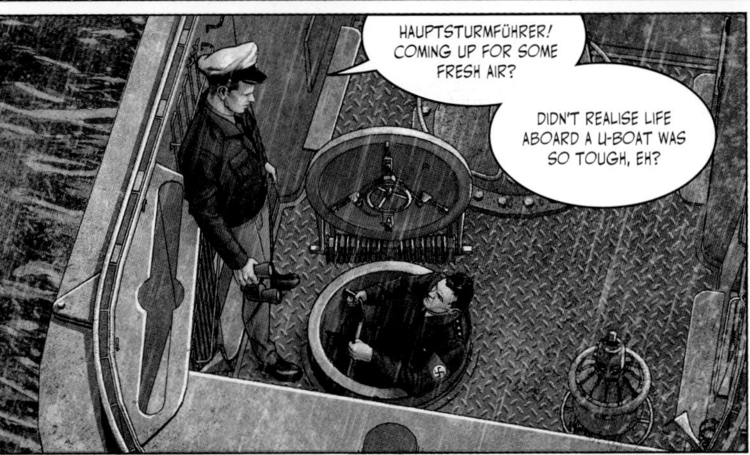
HAUPTSTURMFÜHRER! COMING UP FOR SOME FRESH AIR?
DIDN'T REALISE LIFE ABOARD A U-BOAT WAS SO TOUGH, EH?

QUIT BEING A SMARTASS, WOLFRAM. WHY HAVE WE RESURFACED?
NAVIGATING NON-STOP AT THIS DEPTH IS IMPOSSIBLE.
WE NEED TO REGULARLY REFILL OUR OXYGEN.

YOU HAVE A SNORKEL TO VENTILATE THE DIESEL ENGINES. AND WE COULD SIMPLY STAY TWENTY METERS BELOW THE SURFACE. JUST ENOUGH TO GO UNSEEN.
DESPITE WHAT YOU MAY THINK, I'M BEING EXTREMELY CAUTIOUS.
I'M RARELY USING THE PERISCOPE, AND I ONLY BRING UP THE SUB WHEN STRICTLY NECESSARY. IF YOU TALKED TO MY MEN INSTEAD OF BARKING AT THEM THEY WOULD EVEN TELL YOU I'M A LITTLE PARANOI

BESIDES, WE'RE THREE TIMES FASTER ON THE SURFACE THAN SUBMERGED, AND IT WAS MY UNDERSTANDING THAT THIS WAS AN URGENT MISSION...

STOP BEHAVING LIKE AS ASS!

THE U-864 WAS BUILT AS AN ATTACK VESSEL, *NOT* A CARGO SHIP.
THE U-864 WAS BUILT TO WIN THIS WAR AND SERVE THE REICH.

"I SERVE ADMIRAL DÖNITZ, AND HE HAS ALWAYS TURNED DOWN THESE TRANSPORT MISSIONS. HIS GOAL IS TO WIN THE WAR IN THE ATLANTIC."
"BUT YOU LOST THAT BATTLE, WOLFRAM.
"YOU ACTED LIKE A PACK OF WOLVES. YOU WERE THE MASTERS OF THE SEAS. A NIGHTMARE FOR THE BRITISH, FROM THE MOST LOWLIEST SAILOR TO CHURCHILL HIMSELF..."

BUT NOW YOU'RE NOTHING BUT EASY PREY FOR THE ROYAL NAVY.
YOU LOST THAT BATTLE. HELP US WIN THE WAR.

VRRRR
WHAT THE--?

ALERT!
TAKE US DOWN TO FORTY METERS!
FASTER!
FULL STEAM AHEAD!

ARE WE GOING TO RETALIATE?

QUIET!

STILL NOTHING, COMMANDER.

STAY ON THIS COURSE.
PREPARE TO TAKE US DOWN TO 140 METERS ON MY COMMAND.

UNDERWATER GRENADES!

NOW! TAKE US DOWN TO 140 METERS.

FIND ME THE COORDINATES FOR THOSE GRENADES.

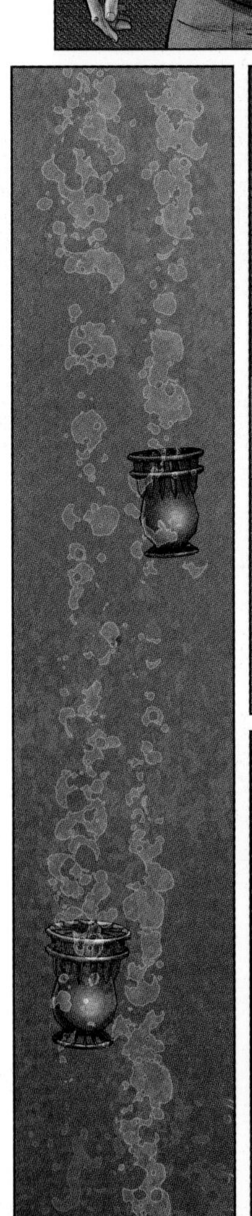

FOURTY-FIVE PERCENT STARBOARD.

NEW TRAJECTORY, 0-6-0.

MAINTAIN COURSE AND SPEED.

I'M NOT GETTING ANY MORE SOUND SIGNATURES.

EXCELLENT.

I WAS RIGHT! YOU'RE GOING TO GET US ALL *KILLED* BY RESURFACING SO OFTEN!
YOU CAN CRITICIZE MY AGE OR MY LOYALTY TO THE REICH AS MUCH AS YOU WANT, HAUPTSTURMFÜHRER...
BUT I'M THE ONLY ONE HERE WHO KNOWS HOW TO COMMAND A U-BOAT. SO YOU'LL JUST HAVE TO TRUST ME.

I ASSURE YOU, THE ALLIED PILOT CAPABLE OF SINKING ME WITH FLOATING GRENADES HASN'T BEEN BORN YET.

WE LOST THEM.
BLAST! NEVER MIND. SEND THEIR LAST COORDINATES TO BASE.

"ONE OF US MIGHT RUN INTO THEM AGAIN... YOU NEVER KNOW."

THE NORTH SEA. SEVERAL HUNDRED KILOMETERS TO THE NORTHWEST.

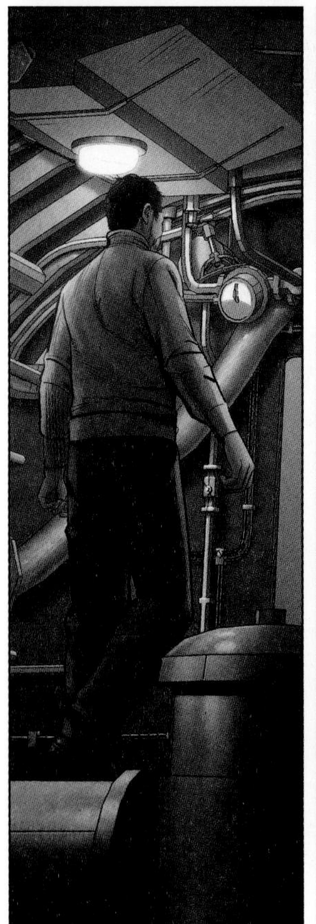

I DIDN'T KNOW IT WAS CUSTOMARY FOR THE CAPTAIN TO SEW THE BOAT'S JOLLY ROGER HIMSELF.

Captain James Launders--HMS Venturer--The Royal Navy.
IT'S NOT, LIEUTENANT. I JUST FIND IT NECESSARY.

NECESSARY?
EVERY STRIPE REPRESENTS AN ENEMY WE SANK. THIRTEEN RED STRIPES, THIRTEEN ENEMY SHIPS.
AND DOZENS OF LIVES LOST EVERY TIME. IT'S OUR MISSION--OUR DUTY--BUT WE MUSN'T FORGET THE LIVES WE TAKE.

BUT I DIDN'T THINK THAT YOU WOULD... ER...
I NEVER HAD YOU DOWN AS SOMEONE WHO WOULD... THIS FLAG IS, ER...
YOU CAN SAY IT... RAISING THIS FLAG JUST BECAUSE, FORTY YEARS AGO, SOME STUPID ADMIRAL CALLED ALL SUBMARINERS PIRATES IS SUPERSTITIOUS.

BUT IT'S A REMINDER OF WHERE WE CAME FROM AND WHO WE ARE.
NOW, DID YOU COME TO SEE ME FOR SEWING ADVICE OR PIRATE STORIES?

NO, CAPTAIN... HQ SENT OVER INFO ON THE COORDINATES OF THAT U-BOAT.
EXCELLENT!

WATSON, PREPARE TO TAKE US DOWN.
AYE, AYE, CAPTAIN.
EMPTY THE BALLAST TANKS!
SO... THE PLANE LOST TRACK OF THE U-BOAT RIGHT HERE, TWO HOURS AGO.
IF IT WERE ME, I WOULD'VE FLED STARBOARD FIRST, THEN CHANGED COURSE TO 1-6-0...

WE SPOTTED A U-BOAT DOING NINETEEN KNOTS PER HOUR. IT HASN'T RESURFACED SINCE. MUST BE HIDING...
I'D HEAD IN THAT DIRECTION. SO IT WOULD MAKE SENSE TO CUT HIM OFF...

WATSON, MAP US OUT A RAPID ROUTE TO THESE COORDINATES.
RIGHT AWAY, CAPTAIN.

CHALMERS, NOTIFY AMBROSE BASE.
TO SAY WHAT? THAT WE'RE GOING WITH A GUT FEELING?

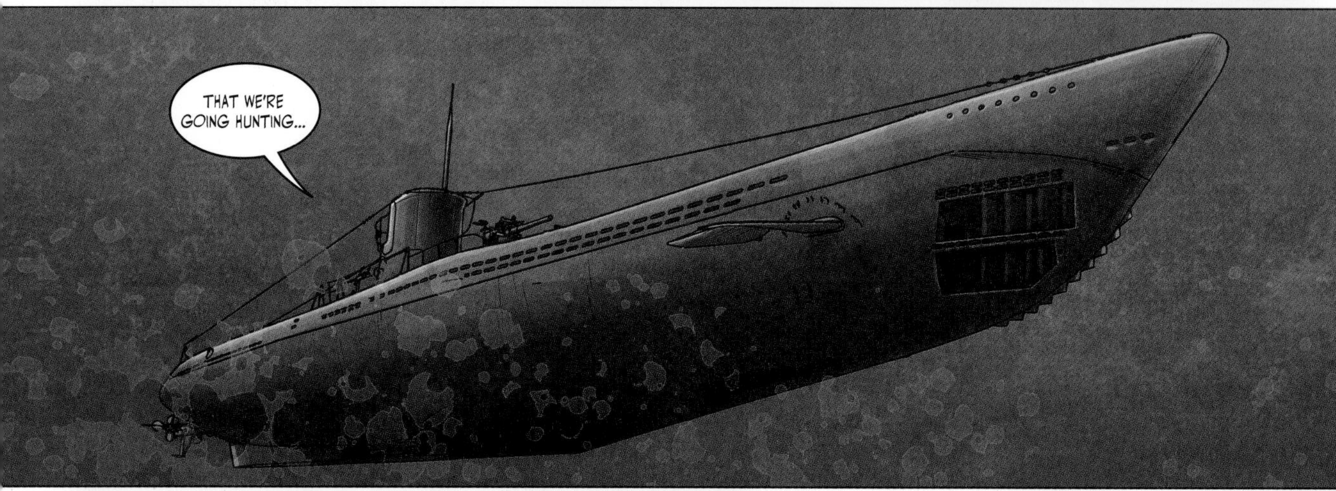
THAT WE'RE GOING HUNTING...

YOU SHOULD FOLLOW KEMMLING'S EXAMPLE, COMMANDER, AND GO GET SOME REST. YOU'VE BEEN ON THE BRIDGE FOR HOURS.
THANK YOU, DIETER, BUT I'LL REST WHEN THE WAR'S OVER.
ARE THE MEN ON FIRST WATCH STILL SLEEPING?

YES. AS PER YOUR ORDERS.
I STILL FIND THAT FASCINATING--KEEPING THE CYCLE OF DAYS AND NIGHTS, EVEN WHILE STUCK DOWN HERE IN THIS TIN CAN...
IT'S WHAT KEEPS US ALIVE--THE ILLUSION OF A NORMAL LIFE...

SONAR ALERT!

I'VE GOT A PROPELLER ON THE HYDROPHONE.
ABOVE OR BELOW THE SURFACE?

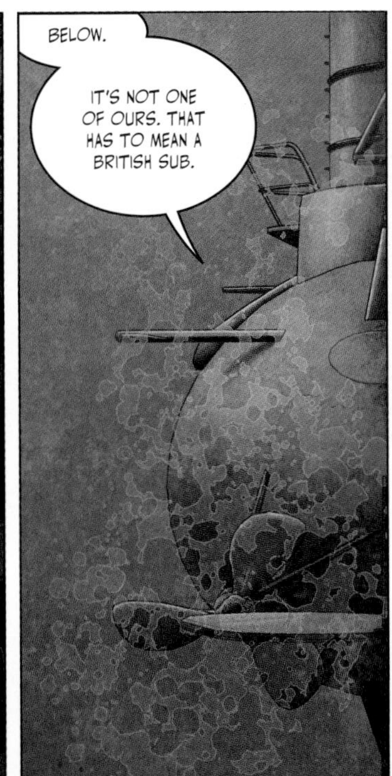
BELOW.
IT'S NOT ONE OF OURS. THAT HAS TO MEAN A BRITISH SUB.

ALL MEN TO YOUR COMBAT POSTS!

GET UP! GET UP! GET UP!
LET'S GO! FASTER!
PROPELLER STILL MOVING AT 2-7-0.
MAINTAIN THIS COURSE.

I THINK IT'S A DUAL PROP, COMMANDER. ONE OF THEIR V-CLASS BOATS.
SMALLER AND SLOWER THAN US.
AND WE OUTGUN THEM...

THE U-BOAT'S MAINTAINING ITS COURSE.

GOOD. DON'T GIVE THEM TIME TO REACT...
LOAD TUBES ONE AND TWO IN CASE THEY GIVE US A CHANCE TO FIRE.

WE HAVE COMPANY? EXCELLENT! LET'S SEE WHAT THE PRIDE OF THE FLEET CAN DO.
WE'RE NOT GOING TO ATTACK. WE'RE GOING TO SHAKE THEM.

WHAT?
A SUBMERGED SUB HAS NEVER BEEN TAKEN DOWN BY ANOTHER SUBMERGED SUB.

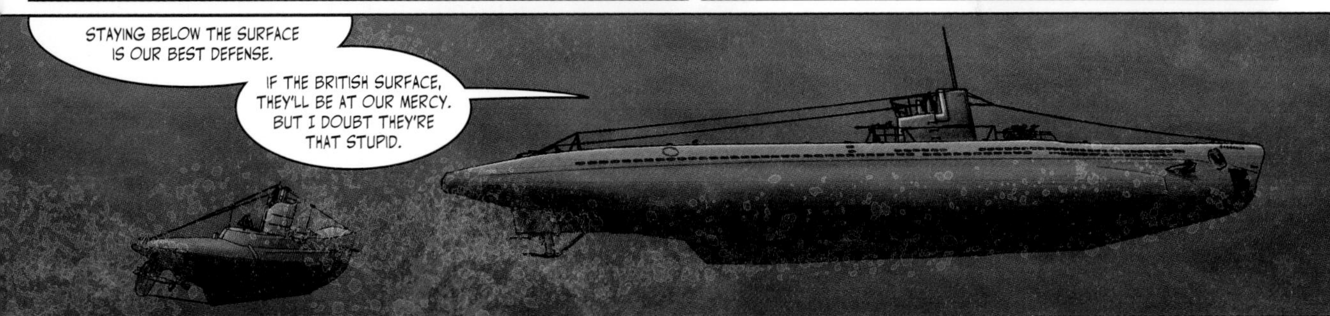
STAYING BELOW THE SURFACE IS OUR BEST DEFENSE.
IF THE BRITISH SURFACE, THEY'LL BE AT OUR MERCY. BUT I DOUBT THEY'RE THAT STUPID.

IT'S OUR *DUTY* TO SHOW FORCE AGAINST THAT TUB!
I THOUGHT OUR DUTY WAS TO RACE AHEAD WITHOUT STOPPING, SO THAT NOTHING CAN HAMPER OUR PRECIOUS MISSION.
SET COURSE TO 2-6-0.

THE U-BOAT'S CHANGED COURSE... IT'S FACING US!
WHAT?

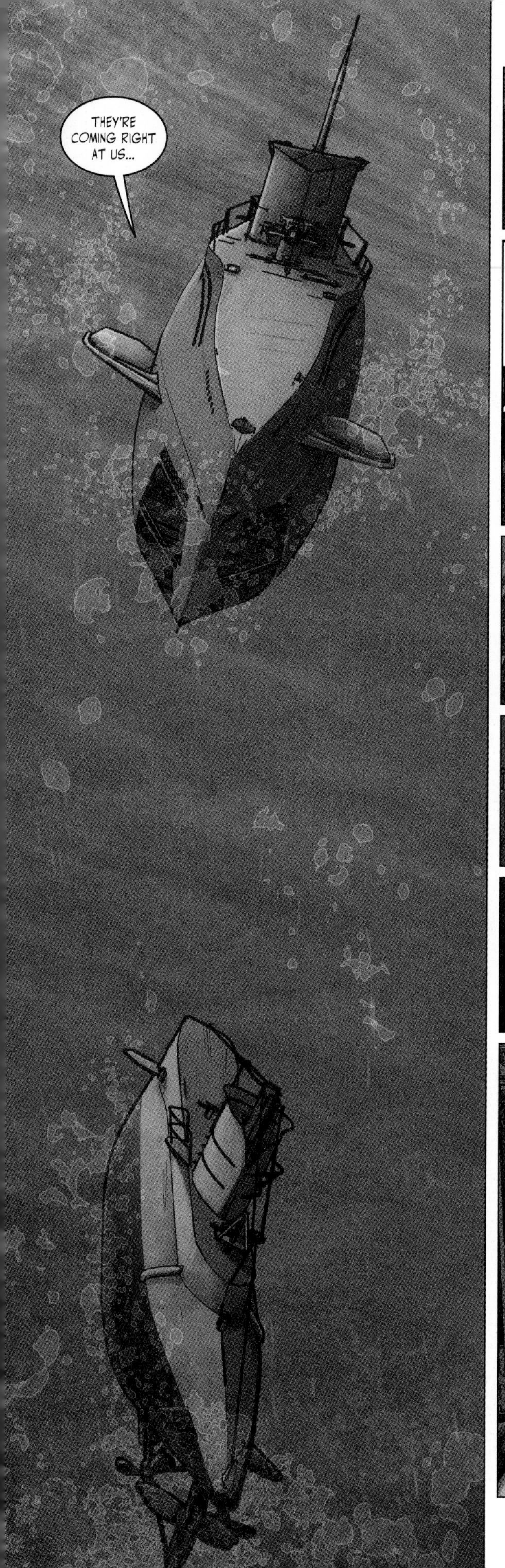
THEY'RE COMING RIGHT AT US...

HAVE THEY LOST THEIR MINDS?

WE'RE FACING THE ENEMY, COMMANDER. THEY'RE MAINTAINING THEIR COURSE.
AS ARE WE.

WHAT ARE THEY TRYING TO PROVE?

WOLFRAM!
COMMANDER?

TWO HUNDRED METERS TO IMPACT, COMMANDER.

EVERYBODY HOLD ON!
VEER TO 2-9-0...
NOW!

WE'RE THROUGH!
BOLLOCKS!

WHAT THE HELL WAS THAT?
WE BRUSHED UP AGAINST A CLIFF.

MAINTAIN COURSE AND MAXIMUM SPEED.

WHERE'D IT GO?
I'VE GOT NOTHING. IT'S BEHIND US NOW.
THE SOUND OF OUR PROPS AND ENGINES ARE DROWNING OUT THEIRS.
THEY'RE FASTER THAN US... BY THE TIME WE TURN AROUND...
I KNOW. THEY'RE LONG GONE... FOR NOW.

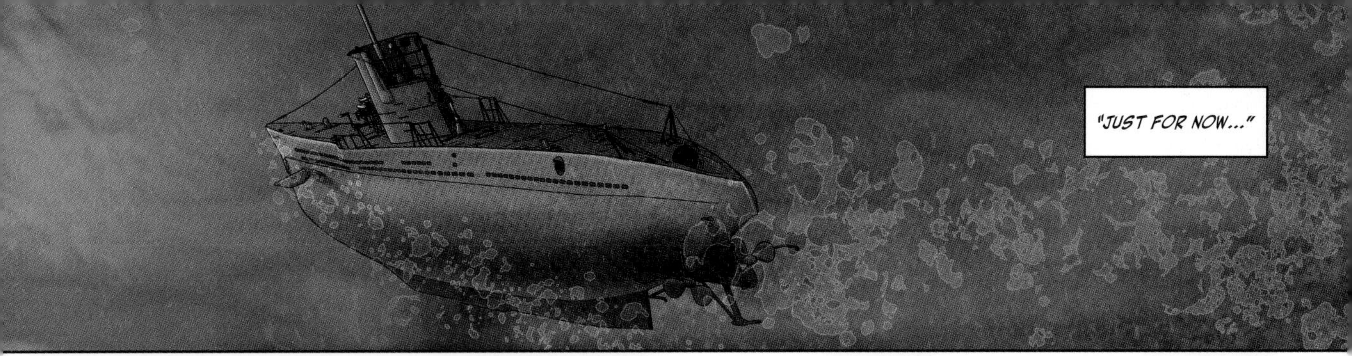
"JUST FOR NOW..."

WHAT'S THE DAMAGE?
A SLIGHT LEAK, BUT WE'VE SEALED IT.
WE'RE NOT SURE IF THE HULL WAS PIERCED OR NOT.

WHAT'S GOING ON, WOLFRAM?

THE SUB'S STILL AIRTIGHT, BUT WE MIGHT HAVE A CRACK IN THE HULL.
WE'LL HAVE TO STOP AT BERGEN TO CHECK IT OUT.

YOU CAN'T BE SERIOUS!
WE DON'T HAVE A CHOICE.
ONCE WE REACH THE ATLANTIC, WE WON'T BE ABLE TO MAKE ANY REPAIRS.

DÖNITZ SHOULD NEVER HAVE ENTRUSTED THIS BOAT TO YOU...

YOU LOOK EXHAUSTED, COMMANDER.
PROBABLY BECAUSE I AM.
HAVE A SEAT, DIETER.
I'LL JUST STAND HERE, COMMANDER.
EVEN NOW, YOU REMAIN FAITHFUL TO POINTLESS TRADITIONS.
I KNOW I'M NOT PERMITTED TO ASK SUCH THINGS, BUT... DO YOU THINK OUR MISSION COULD REALLY--
ALTER THE COURSE OF THE WAR?

HONESTLY, DIETER, I HAVEN'T A CLUE. I DON'T KNOW IF THIS MISSION IS WORTH IT AT ALL. OR IF OUR CARGO WILL EVEN END UP IN THE RIGHT HANDS...
DON'T GET ME WRONG--I'M STILL A PATRIOT. EVEN THOUGH I NEVER WANTED THIS WAR, I'VE ALWAYS WANTED TO SERVE MY COUNTRY.

WHEN WE LOST OUR UPPER HAND IN THE ATLANTIC WAR, THE SS WENT AFTER CAPTAINS THEY THOUGHT WEREN'T STRICT ENOUGH.
ANYONE WHO WASN'T A FANATICAL NAZI WAS KICKED OUT OF THE NAVY... OR EXECUTED.
I LIED SO I COULD KEEP MY POSITION. KEMMLING KNOWS THAT, AND HE WON'T HESITATE TO USE IT AGAINST ME.
BUT THE ONE HOPE I DO STILL HOLD IS TO BRING BACK ALL SEVENTY-TWO MEN IN MY CHARGE.
ANYWAY, THE ONE THING I *DO* KNOW IS THAT THIS CONVERSATION MUST NEVER LEAVE THIS CABIN.
DON'T WORRY ABOUT ME, COMMANDER.
THANK YOU, DIETER.
ASK THE RADIO OFFICER TO SEND AN ENCODED MESSAGE TO THE TOP BRASS.

"HAVE HIM TELL THEM THAT WE'RE MAKING AN UNPLANNED STOP IN BERGEN."

BLETCHLEY PARK,
BUCKINGHAMSHIRE,
ENGLAND.

OPERATION CAESAR
U-864 BERGEN

SCAPA FLOW NAVAL BASE, ORKNEY ISLANDS, SCOTLAND.

SKOLLENBORG, NORWAY.

TO THINK THAT WHEN YOU ARRIVED HERE, YOU HAD NOTHING BUT CONTEMPT FOR YOUR ASSIGNMENT.

YOU DIDN'T WANT TO HELP OUR NETWORK, EVEN THOUGH THE ALTERNATIVE WAS FREEZING YOUR ASS OFF IN ALSACE!

WHAT CAN I SAY, CECILIE...? MEN ALWAYS NEED A LITTLE TIME TO FIGURE THINGS OUT.

TELL YOUR MEN TO BE READY.

THEY ALWAYS ARE.

CAPTAIN, I'VE JUST DECRYPTED SEVERAL MESSAGES SENT BY HQ. THE KIND THAT WEREN'T MEANT FOR US...
CAN YOU CHECK THE DECRYPTION ON THIS ONE?
LET'S SEE IT.

Operation CAESAR,
GOLD, U-864, BERGEN,
NORWAY.

ARE YOU THINKING WHAT I'M THINKING?
YEP. THE GERMANS PUT SIXTY TONS OF GOLD ON A SUB TO ARGENTINA!

SIR? ARE YOU OK?

SEND A MESSAGE TO THE JOINT CHIEFS.
TELL THEM WE RECEIVED THIS MESSAGE BY MISTAKE, BUT THAT WE'LL GLADLY HANDLE THEIR U-BOAT FULL OF GOLD.
YOU WANT US TO GO SINK A SUB?

OF COURSE NOT. FISH WOULDN'T KNOW WHAT TO DO WITH SIXTY TONS OF GOLD.
BUT WE DO.

OK, CHANGE OF PLAN... AGAIN.
BUT THIS IS A GOOD THING. HQ'S GIVING US A MUCH MORE EXCITING MISSION.

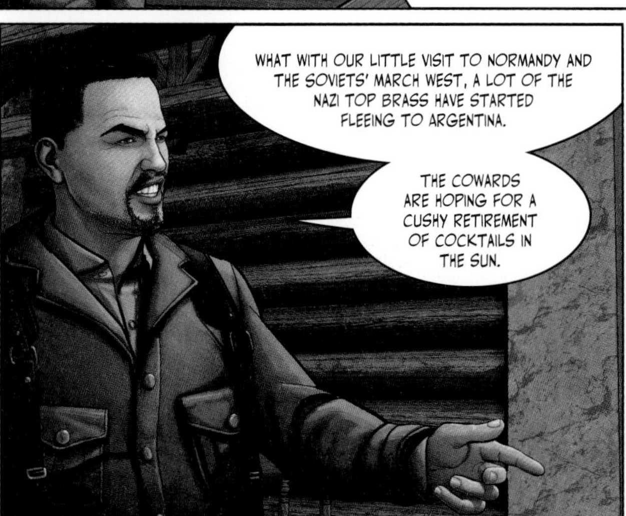
WHAT WITH OUR LITTLE VISIT TO NORMANDY AND THE SOVIETS' MARCH WEST, A LOT OF THE NAZI TOP BRASS HAVE STARTED FLEEING TO ARGENTINA.
THE COWARDS ARE HOPING FOR A CUSHY RETIREMENT OF COCKTAILS IN THE SUN.

AND TO MAKE SURE THEY'RE COMFORTABLE, THEY'RE HAVING SIXTY TONS OF GOLD DELIVERED TO THEM VIA A SUB THAT JUST LEFT GERMANY.

WHAT DOES THIS HAVE TO DO WITH AMERICAN SOLDIERS?

NOBODY WANTS THAT GOLD TO HELP FUND AND ARM THOSE BASTARDS IN OUR BACKYARD.
SO WE'RE GOING TO HELP OURSELVES TO THEIR CARGO AND AVOID DOING WHAT THE BRITS DID--WATCH IT SAIL OUT OF REACH.

WHAT'S WRONG, FITZ?

I'VE HAD IT, CAPTAIN, THAT'S ALL. HOW MANY MORE OF THESE CRAPPY MISSIONS DO WE GET BEFORE THIS WAR IS OVER?

WHAT IF I TOLD YOU THIS WAS THE LAST ONE?

WHAT IF I TOLD YOU WE'RE GONNA *KEEP* THAT GOLD... TO FUND OUR WELL-EARNED RETIREMENT...
WOULD YOU COME BACK INSIDE AND LET ME FINISH MY BRIEFING?

THAT'S ALL WELL AND GOOD, BUT HOW, EXACTLY, DO YOU INTEND TO INTERCEPT A SUBMARINE?
WE DON'T EVEN HAVE A SHIP. WHAT'S YOUR PLAN? TO ASK CECILIE TO GET HER NETWORK TO LOAN US SOME CANOES?

IT'S SIMPLER THAN THAT, WILSON. THE LOOT'S COMING TO *US.*

STILL NO CONTACT.
OKAY...

THE INTEL CHECKS OUT. THEY'RE HEADED FOR BERGEN.
BUT THEY'LL GET THERE BEFORE WE CATCH UP...

SO WE NEED TO SET A TRAP AND SEIZE THE SUB *AFTER* THEY LEAVE THEIR BASE.

HOW MUCH LONGER TILL BERGEN?
A FEW MORE HOURS.

I KNOW YOU'RE NOT USED TO THESE CONDITIONS, BUT THIS ROUTE'S OUR BEST PROTECTION AGAINST GERMAN PATROLS.
WHY DO YOU THINK THE SUB'S DOCKING HERE? THE SOE* COULDN'T SAY.
*SPECIAL OPERATIONS EXECUTIVE--AN ORGANIZATION THAT WAS PART THE BRITISH SECRET SERVICES AND COORDINATED SABOTAGE OPERATIONS IN OCCUPIED COUNTRIES.

NO IDEA. SOME OF THE CREW GOT SICK? TO RESTOCK SUPPLIES? FOR REPAIRS?

WHATEVER THE REASON, THE SUB'LL ONLY BE THERE A FEW HOURS. THE CARGO'S WAY TOO PRECIOUS.
WHICH MEANS WE HAVE A VERY SMALL WINDOW...

HELLO, GORGEOUS.
LOVELY TO MEET YOU.

U-BOAT BUNKER
BRUNO, BERGEN.

WE NEED TO SHIP OUT
OF HERE ASAP.
GET ALL THE
MECHANICS TO INSPECT
THE HULL.

THE TARGET JUST ARRIVED
AT THE BASE.

CECILIE, YOU AND YOUR
TEAM CREATE A DIVERSION
OUTSIDE THE BASE.
MEANWHILE, MY MEN AND I WILL TAKE CARE
OF THE SUB AND GRAB THE CARGO.

THAT WAS
THE PLAN.

YOU'RE REALLY LETTING THEM GO IN ALONE? THEY'RE NOT SOLDIERS... THEY'LL GET SLAUGHTERED.
I DON'T HAVE A CHOICE, FITZ. WE NEED THEM TO DISTRACT THE GUARDS.
I CAN'T LET THEM INTERVENE INSIDE THE BASE. THEY'RE MOSTLY TRAINED IN SABOTAGE. THEY COULD BLOW EVERYTHING UP.

DAMNIT, COLLINS, THEY'RE RESISTANCE FIGHTERS! CIVILIANS!
WHAT HAPPENED TO THE GUY WHO WAS SICK OF SACRIFICING INNOCENT LIVES? DID HE SELL HIS SOUL FOR A FEW GOLD BARS?

THAT GOLD *MUST NOT* LEAVE THE BASE.
AND WHAT'S YOUR PLAN ONCE YOU GET IT? BETRAY YOUR COUNTRY?
GO LIVE THE GOOD LIFE, LIKE A NAZI, IN ARGENTINA?

YOU WANTED A WAY OUT. I FOUND YOU ONE.
YOU'RE NOT A SOLDIER ANYMORE, COLLINS. JUST A CRIMINAL.

CECILIE!

DON'T DO IT! KEEP YOUR GUYS OUT OF THERE. YOU'LL GET YOURSELVES KILLED.
IT'S A RISK WE'RE ALL WILLING TO TAKE, CORPORAL FITZGERALD.
BUT NOT FOR *THIS* REASON. THAT SUB'S CARGO... IT'S *GOLD.* AND COLLINS WANTS IT FOR HIMSELF.

COLLINS?
FITZ, YOU DON'T KNOW WHAT YOU'RE TALKING ABOUT.

SURE I DO.

YOU'RE LOSING IT, MAN!
TELL EVERYBODY WHAT'S ON THAT SUB.

TELL THEM WHAT YOUR PLAN IS FOR THE GOLD.

CORPORAL FITZGERALD! HOLSTER YOUR WEAPON! THAT'S AN *ORDER!*
YOU'VE BETRAYED US ALL. YOU CAN'T GIVE ME ***ORDERS***. TELL THEM WHAT YOUR PLAN IS!

TELL THEM, OR I'LL SHOOT!
FITZ, DON'T MAKE ME...

TELL THEM!

I'M SO SORRY, FITZ... I NEVER THOUGHT IT WOULD COME TO THIS...

THIS WAR CAN MAKE MEN GO CRAZY. WE'VE ALL SEEN IT.
YOU'RE RIGHT. THANK YOU.

IF THERE'S NO HEAVY WATER* ON THAT SUB--LIKE YOU SAID--I'LL FIND OUT.
AND THE NORWEGIAN RESISTANCE *WILL* DO WHAT'S NECESSARY.
*DEUTERIUM OXIDE--A FORM OF WATER THAT CONTAINS ONLY DEUTERIUM RATHER THAN THE HYDROGEN-1 ISOTOPE. IT'S USED IN THE PRODUCTION OF NUCLEAR WEAPONS.

WE HAVE TO--
NO TIME TO BURY HIM, BOSS. WE'LL TAKE CARE OF IT WHEN THE MISSION'S OVER.
FITZ WAS A BROTHER IN ARMS. BUT WE CAN'T LET A GUY WHO'S LOST HIS MARBLES GO ON A MISSION LIKE THIS.
HE WOULD'VE GOT US ALL KILLED.

YOU'RE RIGHT. WE NEED TO GET GOING, OR WE'LL MISS OUR DATE WITH THAT U-BOAT.
WHAT THE HELL IS THAT?

GERMAN FOCKE-WULF 190 FIGHTER PLANES!
THEY MUST BE FROM THE BASE ON HERDLA ISLAND. IT'S FORTY KILOMETERS NORTH OF HERE.

THE BRITS DON'T CARE ABOUT THE CARGO... THEY'RE GONNA SINK THE SUB. I DIDN'T THINK THEY'D GO SO FAR AS TO BOMB THE BASE.
THOSE IDIOTS! WHY WEREN'T WE NOTIFIED?

WE DON'T HAVE MUCH TIME BEFORE THEY START DROPPING BOMBS! LET'S GO! HURRY!
I CAN'T BELIEVE I ACTUALLY HOPE THE LUFTWAFFE STOPS THE AIR RAID!

GET HER BACK IN THE WATER, *ASAP!*

THE MEN ARE GOING AS FAST AS THEY CAN, COMMANDER.
WE NEED TO LEAVE AT ONCE!

THEY'VE STARTED BOMBING ALREADY?
NO. THAT'S SOMETHING ELSE.

ANOTHER ONE?
WAIT FOR THEIR BACKUP TO GET HERE.
*SCHNELLER!**
*SIE SIND DRAUßEN!***
*HURRY!
**THERE THEY ARE!

THEY'VE CLEARED A PATH FOR US.
QUIT GABBING! THE U-BOAT SHOULD BE RIGHT AHEAD OF US.

SHIT! IT'S ALREADY CASTING OFF.

HURRY! LET'S GO!

THAT'S THE ALARM. THE LANCASTERS WERE FASTER THAN I WAS HOPING.
THE BOMBS'LL BE DROPPING ANY SECOND NOW.

WE'RE LEAVING AT ONCE! MAN YOUR STATIONS!

WE NEED TO TAKE COVER.
BEING ON THAT SUB WOULD BE GREAT COVER.

LET'S GO!

RAUS!*
*BEAT IT!

HURRY! WE CAN STILL GET ON BOARD!

THEY GOT AWAY.
NOT YET. WE CAN STILL GO AFTER THEM.
WE NEED TO BOARD BEFORE IT DIVES.

WHAT THE...? THAT'S NOT BOMBS.
NO, THEY'RE DONE BOMBING. THAT'S A MACHINE GUN... OUTSIDE...
CECILIE AND HER MEN. IT'S A MIRACLE THEY'RE STILL ALIVE.

WHAT DO WE DO, CAPTAIN?

WE CAN'T HOLD OUT MUCH LONGER.
I KNOW.

TÖTET SIE ALLE!*
*KILL THEM ALL!

GET IN!

HURRY!

THANKS FOR COMING BACK FOR US.
YOU SCRATCH OUR BACKS...

NOW I KNOW FOR SURE THERE WASN'T ANY GOLD ON THAT SUB.

YOU GOT A PLAN?
WE'RE GONNA TRACK THE TARGET.

HOW LONG UNTILL WE REACH THE MOUTH OF THE BERGEN?

AN HOUR OR SO.
IF THE U-BOAT SURVIVED THE BOMBS, WE'LL BE THERE TO INTERCEPT IT.

MESSAGE FROM HQ, CAPTAIN.

I DON'T *BELIEVE* THIS!

WHAT'S GOING ON?
AN AMERICAN SPECIAL FORCES TEAM HAS SUFFERED CASUALTIES DURING A MISSION WITH THE NORWEGIAN RESISTANCE.
WE'VE BEEN ORDERED TO CHANGE OUR COURSE TO PROVIDE SUPPORT.

CAPTAIN COLLINS?

YEP. AND BOY AM I GLAD TO SEE YOU!
CAPTAIN JAMES LAUNDERS, THE ROYAL NAVY. WELCOME ABOARD HMS VENTURER.

TOLD YOU. IT'S ALL GOING AS PLANNED. THIS IS AN AIRTIGHT COVER.

I HOPE WE WON'T REGRET MAKING THIS DETOUR...

WE'RE CLEAR OF THE PORT'S SHIPPING LANE, COMMANDER.

TAKE US DOWN TO 120 METERS.

DIETER, COME WITH ME.

THE STORM MAY HAVE PASSED, BUT THE CALM WON'T LAST.

HAUPTSTURMFÜHRER KEMMLING'S INTENTIONS WILL LIKELY GO AGAINST THE SUBMARINER CODE OF ETHICS, I'M AFRAID. SO, IN ORDER TO GAIN YOUR FULL TRUST, I'LL TELL YOU EVERYTHING.

WHAT *IS* THAT?

OUR TREASURE.

ENOUGH MERCURY TO PRODUCE THOUSANDS OF BOMBS AND MILLIONS OF ROUNDS. MATERIALS TO MANUFACTURE REVOLUTIONARY WEAPONS.
ENOUGH FOR JAPAN TO GAIN THE UPPER HAND OVER THE AMERICANS... ENOUGH THAT THEY'LL ABANDON EUROPE AND GO HOME...
ENOUGH TO STOP THIS WAR THAT'S GONE ON TOO LONG.

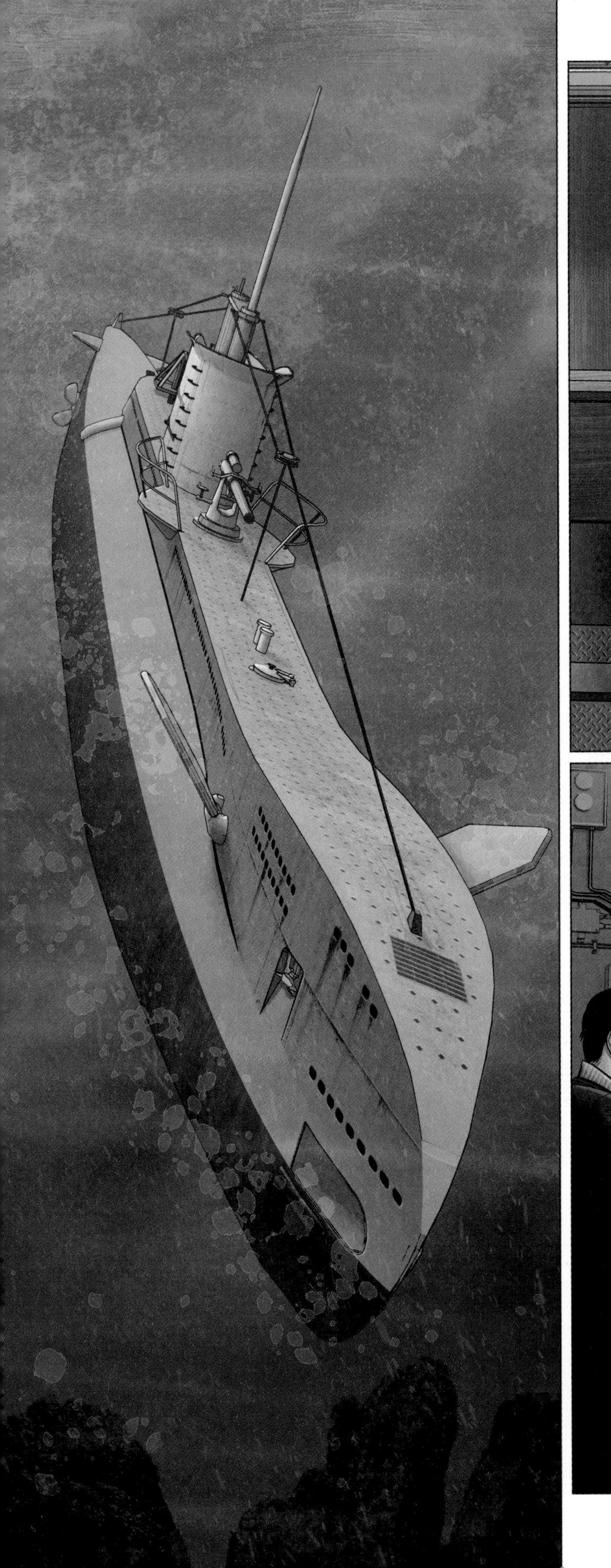

WHAT WERE YOU DOING IN NORWAY?

NOT GOT
ANY COFFEE?

YOU'RE ON A *BRITISH* VESSEL, CAPTAIN.

I'LL NEVER UNDERSTAND YOUR TASTE FOR HOT WATER AND LEAVES...

AND *I'D* LIKE TO UNDERSTAND WHY I WAS ORDERED TO CHANGE COURSE TO PICK UP A BAND OF AMERICAN GRUNTS LOST ON A FJORD...

OUR MISSION WAS TO TRACK A GERMAN SUB, THE U-864. IT GOT AWAY FROM US AT THE BERGEN BASE.

IT'S NOT THE U-BOAT THAT THE U.S ARMY WANTS TO RETRIEVE, BUT ITS CARGO. GENERAL NEWTON PERSONALLY ASKED US TO GET OUR HANDS ON IT AND BRING IT BACK TO HIM.

THE U-864, YOU SAY... WE GOT A RADIO MESSAGE ABOUT THAT, TOO...

I BET THE WHOLE ALLIED FLEET HAS, GIVEN THE NATURE OF THE CARGO.
SO, WILL YOU HELP ME TRACK IT DOWN?

WE ACTUALLY JUST SAW A U-BOAT TO THE SOUTH. BUT WE LOST IT AND FIGURED WE'D FIND IT HERE.
IT HAD TO BE THAT SUB.

BUT FIRST, YOU AND YOUR MEN MUST HAND YOUR WEAPONS OVER TO ME.

THEY'RE NOT ALLOWED ABOARD MY BOAT.

LIEUTENANT CHALMERS, PLEASE TAKE OUR GUESTS' WEAPONS AND LOCK THEM UP.

CAPTAIN COLLINS, I'M COUNTING ON YOUR FULL COOPERATION.

WHY DID YOU TELL HIM THE TRUTH?
BECAUSE WE NEED HIM. DO *YOU* KNOW HOW TO OPERATE A SUBMARINE?

CECILIE AND HER TEAM WOULD NEVER HAVE AGREED TO HELP US IF THEY KNEW THE U-864 WAS CARRYING GOLD AND NOT HEAVY WATER.
BUT LAUNDERS GOT THE SAME MESSAGE WE DID --I CAN'T FOOL HIM.

DON'T WORRY, THOUGH. I KNOW HOW TO HANDLE THAT ARROGANT LIMEY. IF NOT, THERE'S ALWAYS HIS CREW...

IF THINGS DON'T GO AS PLANNED, WAIT FOR MY SIGNAL. YOU'LL KNOW WHAT TO DO.
YES, CAPTAIN.
OUR LAST RECOURSE...

GENERAL NEWTON EXPLICITLY ASKED ME NOT TO LET ANYONE ELSE RETRIEVE THIS CARGO.

WITNESSES BE DAMNED...

THEIR ARMS ARE UNDER LOCK AND KEY.
GOOD.

CAPTAIN...
DO YOU TRUST THAT COLLINS FELLOW?

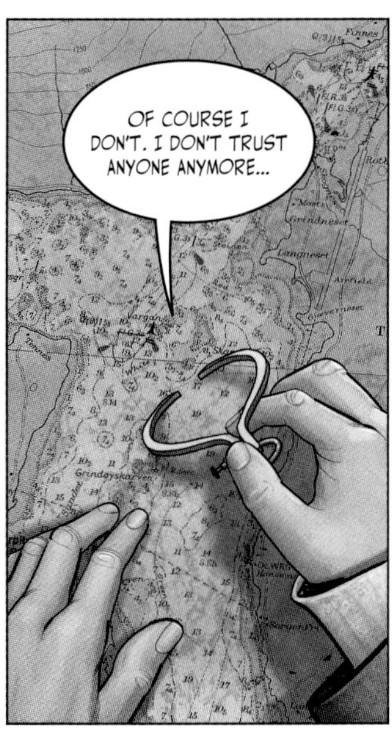
OF COURSE I DON'T. I DON'T TRUST ANYONE ANYMORE...

"...BUT THOSE ARE OUR ORDERS."
FOR NOW, OUR ONLY PRIORITY IS TO FIND THE U-864.

TUBE ONE, FLOODED.
TUBE TWO, FLOODED.

WHAT'S THE ENEMY'S COURSE?

1-1-0, COMMANDER.
RECOMMENDED TRAJECTORY FOR COUNTERATTACK, 2-6-0.
OPEN THE BREACH DOORS!

TUBES ONE AND TWO, OPEN!

HURRY!

COME ON! FASTER!

FASTER... FASTER...

WHAT'S TAKING SO LONG?

CAREFUL! DON'T LET IT SLIP OUT!

TORPEDO, LOADED!

JUNGHANS

FIVE MINUTES...
NOT FAST ENOUGH.

DIETER, HAVE THEM DO THE DRILL AGAIN.
COMMANDER, THE MEN ARE EXHAUSTED.

THE ENEMY DOESN'T CARE. IN WARTIME, YOU'RE EITHER DEAD OR ALIVE. EXHAUSTED IS NOT AN OPTION.
START THE DRILL AGAIN. THEY HAVE TO DO BETTER.

DRAIN TUBES ONE AND TWO.

PREPARE TO REPEAT THE MANEUVER.
AGAIN? IS HE TRYING TO KILL US?

I SEE YOU'RE FINALLY BEING COMBATIVE.
WELL, WE ARE AT WAR, AFTER ALL.

I'M GOING DOWN TO THE ENGINE ROOM.
DIETER, YOU SUPERVISE THE DRILL.

SO, HOW'S OUR GIRL DOING?

WE'VE CHECKED EVERYTHING AGAIN AND AGAIN, LIKE YOU ASKED.
IT'S ALL RUNNING PERFECTLY.

GOOD. LET'S HOPE IT LASTS...

I DON'T WANT ANY MORE SURPRISES.

U-BOATS ENTER BERGEN FROM THE SOUTH AND EXIT FROM THE NORTH...

THAT MEANS THE U-864 MUST'VE HEADED NORTHWEST WHEN IT LEFT THE BASE, TOWARDS FEDJEOSEN--A DEEP CANAL THAT LEADS TO THE OCEAN.

SO... LOGICALLY, THEY'D GO NORTH AROUND THE SHETLAND ISLANDS, THEN WEST OF SCOTLAND.
BUT THOSE ARE DANGEROUS WATERS...

AND THIS IS ALL JUST A GUESS... WHO KNOWS WHAT'S GOING THROUGH THEIR COMMANDER'S HEAD?

I'M GOING TO SOUND LIKE AN IDIOT, BUT...

HOW *DOES* ONE CLIMB ABOARD A SUBMARINE?
YOU HAVE TO FORCE IT TO SURFACE OR WAIT FOR IT TO COME UP.

YOU CAN'T SINK IT WHILE IT'S SUBMERGED. IT'S NEVER BEEN DONE.

I'LL TAKE THAT AS GOOD NEWS. SINKING IT AND LEAVING THE CARGO AT THE BOTTOM OF THE OCEAN IS OUT OF THE QUESTION.

BEFORE WE DECIDE WHAT TO DO, FIRST WE HAVE TO FIGURE OUT HOW TO FIND IT IN ALL THIS WATER...

WE CAN'T. NOT UNLESS WE GET *VERY* LUCKY. WE'D NEED A SPY PLANE TO FIND IT.

BUT I'M POSITIVE THEY WON'T RISK TRANSITING ON THE SURFACE AGAIN-- NOT NOW THAT THEY KNOW THEY'RE BEING HUNTED...

I MIGHT HAVE AN IDEA...

WOULD I BE PERMITTED TO SEND A MESSAGE TO AN OLD FRIEND?

MESSAGE SENT.

THANK YOU. AND CAN YOU SEND THIS ONE TO GENERAL NEWTON? YOUR CAPTAIN AUTHORIZED IT.

IS THIS WHERE YOU'RE GOING AFTER WE WIN THE WAR?

YEP. IF I EVER HAVE ENOUGH MONEY!

WHAT THE HELL ARE YOU DOING? TEAMING UP WITH THEM AND HOPING THEY'LL ACCEPT THEIR SHARE OF THE LOOT WITH A SMILE?
RELAX, WILSON. I KNOW WHAT I'M DOING.

PLUS, IF WE HAVE TO START A MUTINY TO KEEP THE CARGO, IT'S GOOD TO START MAKING FRIENDS...

YOU WANTED TO SEE ME?

WE HAVEN'T SPOKEN ABOUT THE MISSION, AND THE CARGO, SINCE YOU SHOWED IT TO ME, COMMANDER.

YOU EXPRESSED YOUR DOUBTS TO ME AND... WELL... I'M HAVING MORE AND MORE OF THEM MYSELF...

DIETER, WE CAN'T DISCUSS THIS IN THE OPEN. THERE ARE EYES AND EARS EVERYWHERE...

COMMANDER, IF WE DELIVER THE MERCURY TO THE JAPANESE, THIS WAR WILL *NEVER* END.

I KNOW.
I'M ALSO WONDERING WHAT THE BEST COURSE OF ACTION IS. PURSUE THIS MISSION, SURRENDER TO THE ALLIES, OR SINK THE SUB WHERE NOBODY WILL COME LOOKING FOR IT... WAIT...
WHAT THE--?

WHAT'S GOING ON?
ENEMY FRIGATES ON THE SURFACE, COMMANDER!
HOW MANY?
TWO, I THINK. THEY CAN'T BE MORE THAN A FEW MILES AWAY.
STOP THE ENGINES!
"STOP THE ENGINES!"

COULD THEY HAVE HEARD US BEFORE WE STOPPED?

WE WERE IN THEIR WAKE, SO I DON'T THINK SO.
THE SOUND OF THEIR OWN ENGINES WOULD HAVE DROWNED OUT OURS.

WHEN WILL WE KNOW IF THEY DETECTED US?

THAT'S NOT WHAT WORRIES ME.

A SUBMARINE CAN'T STOP IN THE WATER. IT KEEPS GLIDING.
WE HAVE TO HOPE WE CAN RESTART OUR ENGINES ASAP, AND THAT NOTHING GETS IN OUR WAY.

DO YOU WANT TO GO UP TO PERISCOPE DEPTH TO MAKE SURE?
IT'S TOO DANGEROUS. EVEN FROM A FEW MILES AWAY, THEIR LOOK-OUTS COULD SPOT OUR PERISCOPE.

OPERATOR, GIVE ME THEIR POSITION AGAIN!

I HEAR MOVEMENT...

THEY'RE STILL AT 1-8-5. THEY'RE CONTINUING ON THEIR WAY!

EXCELLENT...

START THE ENGINES AND TAKE US UP TO TWENTY METERS.

WE MIGHT MAKE A FIGHTER OF YOU YET. I ALMOST THOUGHT YOU WERE GOING TO RAM THEM!
WE WON'T BE ATTACKING ANYONE. THAT'S NOT OUR MISSION.

YES. THE MISSION COMES FIRST.

YOU'VE HAD US SAILING UP THE COAST FOR THREE DAYS, CAPTAIN!
AND *STILL* NO SIGN OF THE U-864...

DID YOU THINK IT'D BE EASY TO FIND ONE U-BOAT IN THE VASTNESS OF THE OCEAN?
STILL NO RESPONSE FROM YOUR NORWEGIAN FRIENDS...
YOU'RE NOT THRILLED ABOUT ME BEING HERE, ARE YOU?
YOU REMIND ME OF SOMEONE I USED TO KNOW...
SO I'M WARY.
DON'T YOU HAVE ANYTHING MORE SOPHISTICATED THAN THESE BINOCULARS AND OUR OWN EYES TO SPOT THEM?
THE SEARCH AREA IS HUGE, WE'RE USING EVERYTHING WE HAVE AVAILABLE.
BUT I DON'T WANT TO TAKE ANY UNNECESSARY RISKS, LIKE USING THE ASDIC* WHILE WE'RE SUBMERGED.
WE'D GIVE AWAY OUR PRESENCE AND OUR POSITION.
*ASDIC: A SONAR USED TO DETECT SUBMARINES.
OUR RADIOMAN CAN ONLY USE HIS HYDROPHONE TO T
TO DETECT THE SOUND O
PROPELLERS.
SO PRAY THAT FATE LENDS US A HAND.

COME IN,
KEMMLING.

SIT DOWN,
FOR ONCE.

THOSE FRIGATES ARE LONG GONE BY NOW. WHY AREN'T YOU CRANKING UP THE ENGINES?

THESE WATERS AREN'T SAFE. WE NEED TO TAKE THEM SLOW AND STEADY.

I DON'T WANT TO RUN INTO ANOTHER ENEMY SUB.
OR FIND OUT HOW MANY SHIPS THE ROYAL NAVY HAS DEPLOYED AROUND NORWAY.

COMMANDER! COME QUICKLY!
ANOTHER SONAR ALERT?

NO. IT'S COMING FROM THE ENGINE ROOM!

IT HAPPENED ALL OF A SUDDEN, COMMANDER! THERE WAS A HUGE EXPLOSION!
IN THE CYLINDER OR THE COMPRESSOR?
WE DON'T KNOW YET.

BUT WHEREVER IT IS, WE CAN'T REPAIR IT HERE.

WE HAVE A PROBLEM WITH THE PISTONS IN THE AIR COMPRESSOR.

WE CAN'T RUN THE ENGINES AT MORE THAN THIRTY PERCENT CAPACITY.

MEANWHILE, WE'RE MAKING ONE HELL OF A RACKET.

SEND THE FOLLOWING MESSAGE AT ONCE: "U-864 ENGINE FAILURE.

"REQUEST URGENT INSTRUCTIONS."
COMMANDER! COMMANDER!

YOU HAVE TO SEE THIS.

THIS IS WHAT CAUSED THE DAMAGE?
YES... DEFINITELY! AND IT'S TOO CLEAN A CUT TO HAVE BEEN AN ACCIDENT...

I HAVE AN ANSWER FROM HQ, COMMANDER.

WE'RE TO RETURN TO BERGEN. THEY'RE SENDING AN ESCORT. IT'LL BE HERE IN THREE DAYS...
IF WE'RE STILL ALIVE...

U-BOAT BUNKER BRUNO, BERGEN. FEBRUARY 1945.
PICK UP THE PACE!
I CAN'T WAIT TILL THEY'RE DONE REPAIRING THE BASE.
I'M SICK OF BABYSITTING THESE ANIMALS.

NOW!

AARRGGH! MY LEG!

GET UP! NOW!

I CAN'T... TOO COLD... CAN'T FEEL... MY HANDS...

GET UP, OR YOU'RE USELESS TO US.
AND YOU KNOW WHAT HAPPENS TO PEOPLE WHO HAVE NO USE...

U 864

FINALLY!

FREEZE! YOU THINK WE DIDN'T NOTICE YOUR LITTLE TRICK?

ON YOUR KNEES! NOW!

YOU'LL PAY FOR THAT...

SPILL IT!

I'M TELLING YOU THE TRUTH! I DIDN'T DO IT!

HAUPTSTURMFÜHRER! LET GO OF THAT MAN!

I'M JUST DOING MY JOB.
WE HAVE A TRAITOR ONBOARD THIS BOAT. WE MUST FIND HIM.

I AM THE SOLE AUTHORITY ABOARD THIS VESSEL. I WILL CARRY OUT ANY NECESSARY INVESTIGATION.
YOU SHOULD HAVE STARTED A LONG TIME AGO. BEFORE WE ENDED UP IN THIS SITUATION.

THIS IS MY SUBMARINE. EVERYBODY ABIDES BY MY RULES.

IT'S ONLY YOURS IF IT'S STILL IN ONE PIECE...

SPEAKING OF FATE, IT'S GIVEN US A LITTLE PRESENT...

IT BROKE DOWN?
HIGHLY UNUSUAL. SOMETHING MUST'VE HAPPENED ON BOARD.

YOU CAN THANK YOUR OLD FRIEND WHEN YOU SEE HER.
WHO CARES...? AS LONG AS IT WORKS IN OUR FAVOR.

YES...

QUICK SWERVE TO STARBOARD. COURSE TO 2-6-0. FULL STEAM AHEAD.

THANKS. GOOD JOB.
JUST DOING MY DUTY.

BUT IT DOESN'T BUY THE DREAM LIFE IN PARADISE, DOES IT? ALWAYS THE SAME OLD STORY FOR GUYS LIKE US...
WELL, NOT *ALWAYS*...

IF YOUR INTEL'S RELIABLE, THE U-864 SHOULD BE CLOSE BY.
SO NOW WHAT? WE PLAY HIDE AND SEEK WITH THEM?
WE SHUT UP AND WE LISTEN.
STAY ON THE HYDROPHONE. DON'T SWITCH TO THE ASDIC.
I KNOW YOU CAN DO THIS. FIND THAT SUB.
I'M GETTING A FAINT SOUND AT 1-3-5. COULD BE AN ENGINE.
CHALMERS, TAKE US UP TO PERISCOPE DEPTH. SET HELM TO 1-3-5.
ARE YOU SURE? THEY COULD SPOT US.
I KNOW, BUT I NEED TO BE SURE.

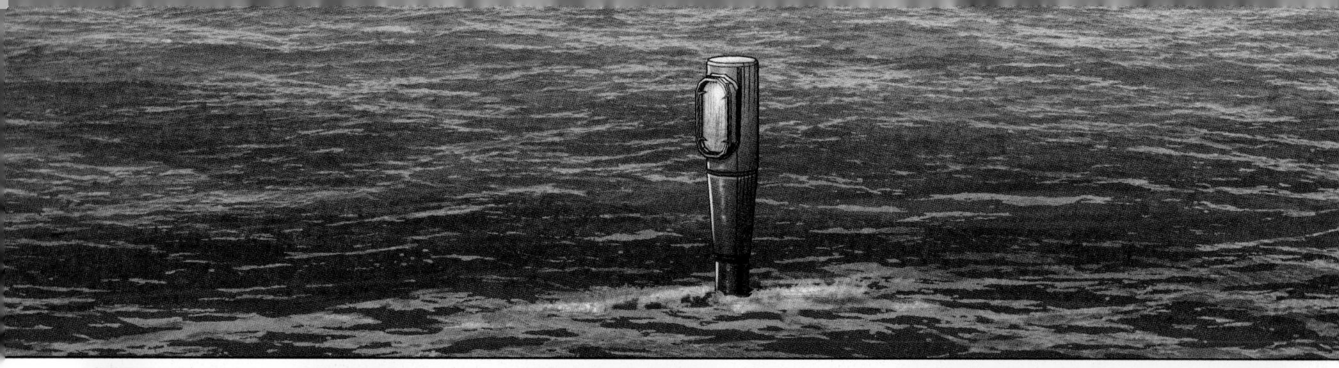

NOTHING... COULD'VE BEEN A FISHING BOAT...
TAKE HER DOWN AGAIN?

NO. WE DIDN'T COME ALL THIS WAY TO NOT FIND THAT SUB.
WE STAY HERE AND WE WAIT.

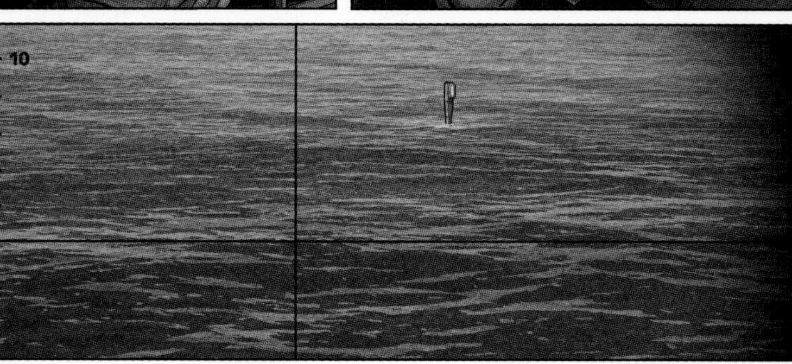
OVER THERE! I THINK I HAVE SOMETHING.
10

OPERATOR, CHECK WITH HQ TO SEE IF THERE ARE ANY ALLIED SUBS IN THE AREA.

WHAT DO YOU THINK YOU SAW?
COULD'VE BEEN A PERISCOPE... NO, IT *HAD* TO BE A PERISCOPE.

CAPTAIN, HQ CONFIRMS THAT WE'RE THE ONLY SUB FOR MILES.

THEN IT HAS TO BE A U-BOAT.

THE GAME'S AFOOT!

TAKE US DOWN TO FIFTY METERS.

WE'RE MAKING FAR TOO MUCH NOISE.
WE DON'T HAVE A CHOICE, COMMANDER, IF WE WANT TO MEET OUR ESCORT.

IT'S *STILL* NOT HERE? CAN'T WE GO ANY FASTER?
THE FASTER WE GO, THE LOUDER OUR ENGINES GET.
AND I DON'T WANT TO GET THERE BEFORE THE ESCORT. WE'D BE SITTING DUCKS.

NOW, KEEP OUT OF THE WAY AND LEAVE THIS TO ME.
WE'LL STAY AT THIS SPEED AND GO UP TO PERISCOPE DEPTH TO CHECK FOR THE ESCORT.

JUST PRAY THAT AN ENEMY PLANE DOESN'T SPOT US. AS LONG AS WE STAY UNDERWATER, WE'RE SAFE.

CHALMERS, KEEP GOING SLOW. I DON'T WANT THEM TO KNOW WE'RE HERE.

SONAR, I WANT READINGS ON THE SUB'S POSITION EVERY TWO MINUTES.

ARE ALL THE READINGS AND THE CALCULATIONS SO YOU DON'T LOSE THEM, OR SO YOU CAN FIRE AT THEM?
I TOLD YOU, FIRING WHILE THE SUB IS SUBMERGED IS NOT AN OPTION. IT'S NEVER BEEN DONE BEFORE.
AND SO FAR, THEY'RE ONLY GOING UP AS FAR AS PERISCOPE DEPTH.

"THERE ARE NO RULES FOR THIS SITUATION, SINCE THERE'S NO PRECEDENT.
"SUBS ARE BUILT TO TRACK TARGETS ON THE SURFACE, NOT TO ENGAGE IN COMBAT WITH ANOTHER SUB.
"UNDERWATER, THE HUNTER AND THE PREY ARE BOTH BLIND, SO HOW CAN WE TELL WHICH ONE WE ARE?"

IF I FIRE AND MISS, THEY CAN CALCULATE THE TORPEDOES' POINT OF ORIGIN AND FIRE BACK.

SO FOR NOW, WE'LL JUST STAY ON THEM.

NOTHING ON THE HYDROPHONE YET?
IT'S HARD TO HEAR ANYTHING OVER THE SOUND OF OUR ENGINES...

HOLD ON. I'VE GOT SOMETHING!

A PROPELLER... IT'S COMING FROM BEHIND US. AN ENEMY SUB!

SET THE HELM TO 1-8-0 FOR THIRTY SECONDS.
THEN SET IT TO 2-9-0 FOR A ZIGZAG TRAJECTORY.

THE U-BOAT JUST CHANGED ITS COURSE.

I THINK IT'S STARTING TO ZIGZAG.

DIETER, TAKE US UP TO PERISCOPE DEPTH.
IT'S ONLY 2,500 METERS FROM US NOW, CAPTAIN! AND IT'S GOING UP!
HIS TRAINING'S KICKING IN. NOW IT'S ALL ABOUT WHO SPOTS THE OTHER FIRST.
"HE'S LOOKING FOR US.
"BUT HE SHOULDN'T BE...
"HIS INSTINCT IS TELLING HIM TO LOOK FOR THE HUNTER. THE LOGICAL APPROACH WOULD BE TO HIDE.
"BUT IT'S INSTINCTIVE TO WANT TO SEE YOUR ENEMY.
"IF HE SEES US, HE'S NOT THE PREY ANYMORE. HE THINKS THIS'LL MAKE HIM THE HUNTER..."

TAKE US BACK DOWN TO SIXTY METERS AND SET A COURSE FOR A CONSTANT ZIGZAG TRAJECTORY.

COMMANDER, I NEED TO SPEAK WITH YOU...
ALONE.

I DON'T UNDERSTAND WHAT YOU'RE DOING.
I'M TRYING TO KEEP US *ALIVE!* YOU AND ME, AND *ALL* THE MEN IN MY CHARGE!

YOU TOLD ME YOU WERE QUESTIONING OUR MISSION, AND THAT WE HAD TO GET RID OF THE CARGO...
I SABOTAGED THE ENGINE TO ENABLE YOU TO DO JUST THAT. BUT YOU'RE GOING ON AS IF NOTHING HAPPENED.

WHAT DID YOU DO, DIETER?!

I GAVE YOU THE CHANCE TO RESURFACE AND SURRENDER THIS BOAT TO THE BRITISH.

HAVE YOU LOST YOUR MIND?

IT'S THE ONLY WAY TO STOP THE WAR, YOU SAID SO YOURSELF.
IT'S WHAT YOU WANTED...
I SAID I HAD DOUBTS! THAT'S ALL!

BUT HE TOOK YOU AT YOUR WORD, COMMANDER.

THERE ARE EYES AND EARS EVERYWHERE DOWN HERE.

KEMMLING, HOLSTER THAT WEAPON!
YOU THINK YOU'RE IN CHARGE OF THIS VESSEL, BUT I ALONE AM RESPONSIBLE FOR THIS MISSION!

AND THIS TRAITOR JEOPARDIZED IT.

NO!

CAPTAIN! I HEARD A *GUNSHOT!*

SOMEONE OPENED FIRE IN THAT TIN CAN?

YOU WERE RIGHT. SOMETHING ODD *IS* HAPPENING ABOARD THAT BOAT...
I'M MOSTLY WORRIED ABOUT THEIR TRAJECTORY. IT MEANS THEY KNOW WE'RE AFTER THEM.

"AND EVERY TURN PUTS THEM IN A BETTER POSITION TO FIRE ON US.

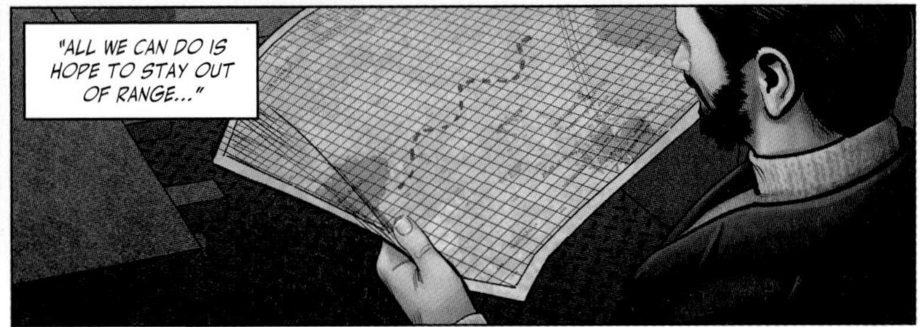
"ALL WE CAN DO IS HOPE TO STAY OUT OF RANGE..."

HE WAS A TRAITOR AND A COWARD.

HE GOT THE DEATH HE DESERVED.

THEY'D GET TO THE PORT FASTER BY KEEPING IN A STRAIGHT LINE.
THAT WOULD MAKE THEIR COURSE TOO PREDICTABLE.
WITHOUT AN ESCORT, THEIR ONLY CHANCE IS TO KEEP ON THE MOVE.

THEY WON'T RESURFACE.... WHICH LEAVES ME NO OTHER OPTION... WE HAVE TO ATTACK FIRST.

YOU CAN'T DO THAT! WE HAVE TO RETRIEVE THE CARGO *INTACT.*
I DIDN'T RECEIVE THE SAME ORDERS YOU DID. MINE WERE TO SINK THAT SUB...AT *ALL* COSTS...

REGARDLESS OF THE MERCURY OR THE WEAPON BLUEPRINTS IT'S TRANSPORTING.

WHAT'S WRONG? WHAT DID YOU HOPE TO FIND ON THAT U-BOAT?
SIXTY TONS OF GOLD? MARLENE DIETRICH? EVA BRAUN?

I NEED TO GET A MESSAGE TO GENERAL NEWTON. RIGHT AWAY!

I DON'T UNDERSTAND YOUR ENCRYPTION METHOD...
THAT'S THE IDEA.
THE RESPONSE WILL BE ENCRYPTED, TOO. DON'T GET A SINGLE CHARACTER WRONG.

WHAT'S WRONG, BOSS?
THEY TOOK US FOR IDIOTS.

CAPTAIN COLLINS! YOUR ANSWER.

DAMNIT! THAT ASSHOLE!

WHAT DID THE GENERAL SAY?
THERE WAS NEVER ANY GOLD ON THAT U-BOAT. HE LIED TO GET US TO ACCEPT THE MISSION.
THEY WANTED TO MAKE SURE WE'D BRING THE CARGO BACK INTACT AND NOT LET THE BRITS DESTROY THE SUB.

SO WE'RE NOT ALLIES WITH THE BRITS NOW?
IT'S NOT A MATTER OF NOW, BUT OF AFTER. THE BRITS WANT TO END THIS WAR AS SOON AS POSSIBLE...
BUT WASHINGTON IS ALREADY PLANNING THE NEXT PHASE. ONCE THE GERMANS ARE NO LONGER A THREAT, IT'LL BE TIME TO ARM UP TO FIGHT THE ROOSKIES.

THE GENERAL'S MESSAGE WAS CLEAR--WE HAVE TO FIND A WAY TO BRING BACK THAT MERCURY...
AND AVOID ITS DESTRUCTION AT ALL COSTS.

DESTRUCTION?

DESTRUCTION.

TELL ME WE'RE GOING TO TAKE OUT THE WHOLE CREW!

ONLY THOSE WHO REFUSE TO COOPORATE.

I NEVER THOUGHT IT'D COME TO THIS...
I DID.

REMEMBER MY OFFER? YOU STILL WANT TO RETIRE IN PARADISE?
TIME TO PICK A SIDE, BUDDY.

I'M IN!

THEY'RE UNDER HERE.

THE ONLY PLACE WE DIDN'T THINK TO SEARCH...

TAKE ADAMS AND JONES, AND SECURE THE AFT OF THE SUB.
WILSON AND I WILL TAKE THE BRIDGE.

STOP YOUR FIRING MANEUVERS, LAUNDERS. YOU'RE NOT LAUNCHING ANY TORPEDOES.

AND WHO'LL COMMAND THIS SUB IF YOU SHOOT ME?
MAYBE YOUR XO WILL BE MORE COMPLIANT.

WE DON'T HAVE ANY CHOICE BUT TO ATTACK, *NOW.*
THEY'RE HEADING TO THE LIGHTHOUSE ON FEDJE. ONCE THEY PASS IT, WE'VE LOST THEM.

I KNOW WHERE THEY'RE GOING...
AND I WON'T LET YOU ATTEMPT SOMETHING THAT'S NEVER BEEN DONE BEFORE.
THERE'S A FIRST TIME FOR EVERYTHING.

FOLLOW THEM BACK TO BERGEN!
WE CAN ATTACK THEM ON LAND, AND GRAB THE CARGO.

YOU'LL HAVE TO SHOOT ME.
BUT WHAT KIND OF MORON FIRES A WEAPON ON A SUBMARINE?

YOU'RE GOING TO MISS BEING ABLE TO WALK...

CLIC
CLIC

WHAT THE...?

I FIGURED YOU'D TRY SOMETHING LIKE THIS SOONER OR LATER...

I NEVER TRUST DAREDEVILS...

TAKE THEM TO THE BRIG!

"IT'S GAME OVER FOR THEM."

FIND THAT ENEMY SUB!
KEMMLING! GET YOUR HANDS OFF MY PERISCOPE!

YOU ARE NO LONGER IN CONTROL OF THIS BOAT.

HE DOES THIS... CALCULATES ALL THE TRAJECTORIES OVER AND OVER.

THE ZIGZAGS FOLLOW A PATTERN! A DEVIATION OF FIFTEEN DEGREES EVERY TEN MINUTES...

"IT'S OUR ONLY CHANCE. BUT IT'S NOT CERTAIN...
"AS SOON AS WE FIRE, THEY'LL KNOW ABOUT IT. THEY'LL CHANGE TACK AND HAVE TIME TO RESPOND..."
WE'VE BEEN FOLLOWING THEM FOR THREE HOURS. THEY'RE NOT RESURFACING.
WE'RE GOING TO HAVE TO FIRE BLIND. WE'LL NEED TO PLOT THEIR POSITION DOWN TO THE LAST CENTIMETER...
WHEN WILL YOU BE READY?
TWO HOURS... MAYBE THREE. IN THE MEANTIME, HAVE THEM LOAD THE TUBES.
WE'RE NEVER GETTING OUT OF HERE...
ALL THIS WORK, ALL THOSE DREAMS... JUST TO END UP IN A DAMN CELL...
CHALMERS, THE U-BOAT WILL BE AT THESE COORDINATES IN TWO MINUTES. LET'S NOT MISS OUR WINDOW.
ALL FOUR TUBES ARE READY. WE'RE JUST AWAITING YOUR ORDERS.
ON MY COMMAND...

I'VE GOT SOMETHING AT 1-8-0. DIRECTLY BEHIND US!
IT'S A TORPEDO!
FORWARD HELM HARD TO PORT! PITCH MINUS FIFTEEN! DIVE DOWN TO 100 METERS!
I WANT ONE EVERY SEVENTEEN SECONDS, CHALMERS.
FIRE TUBE THREE. THEN HELM TO 0-1-15, PITCH MINUS TEN.
I HOPE THIS IS THE RIGHT CALL, CAPTAIN...
"ONCE WE FIRE OUR FOURTH TORPEDO, WE'LL BE COMPLETELY DISARMED."
"I HOPE SO, TOO... IF I'M WRONG, THEY'LL KNOW EXACTLY WHERE WE ARE... AND THEY HAVE 22 TORPEDOES TO FIRE AT US..."
HE DID IT... HE'S FIRED ON THE GERMANS.
FIRE TUBE FOUR!
NOW, TAKE US DOWN.
THREE MORE TORPEDOES ON APPROACH, COMMANDER!

WHAT'S THEIR TRAJECTORY?
2,500 METERS AWAY, TO 1-7-0.
HELM TO 2-8-0, DIVE THIRTY METERS.
1.44. 1.56. 1.57...
THEY'VE DODGED THE FIRST ONE.
THAT WAS TO BE EXPECTED.
WE HAVE TO FIRE BACK, WOLFRAM!
SHUT UP AND LET ME GET US OUT OF THIS!
HELM TO 1-6-5!
THE SECOND TORPEDO'S MISSED.

THEY'VE DODGED THE THIRD ONE!
SO FAR, HE'S DONE EXACTLY WHAT HE WAS SUPPOSED TO DO.
JUST AS I ANTICIPATED.
THE FOURTH TORPEDO'S COMING STRAIGHT AT US!
GOOD GOD...

I'LL HAVE NO CELEBRATING... THEY WERE SUBMARINERS JUST LIKE US, AND NOW THEY'RE DEAD.
"MAY NEPTUNE WELCOME THEM INTO HIS ETERNAL KINGDOM..."

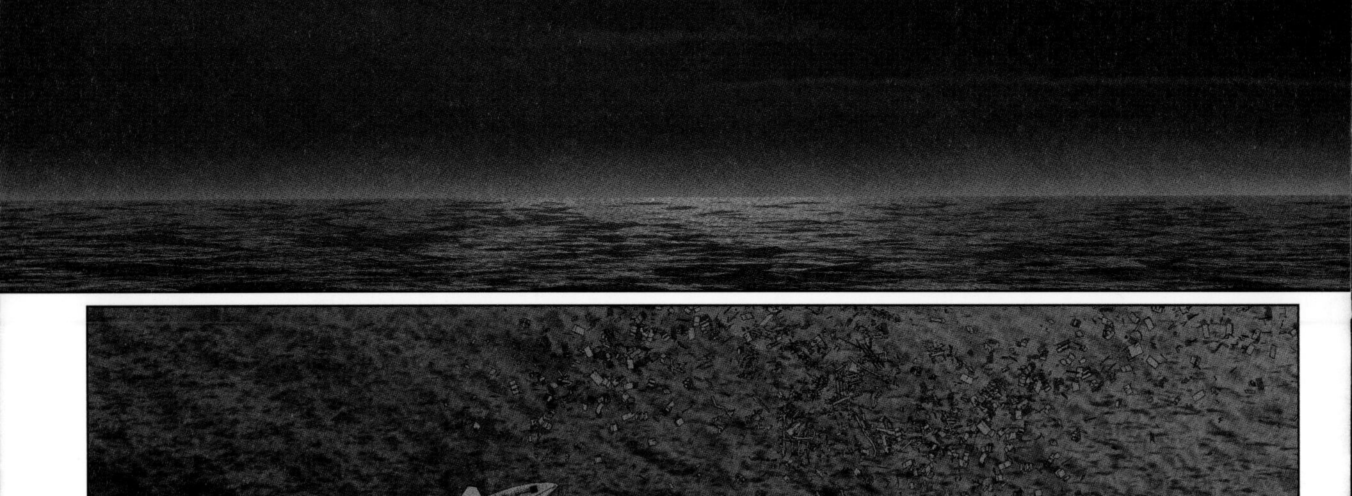

YOU WANTED TO SEE ME?
RELAX, COLLINS. YOU'RE NOT A PRISONER ANYMORE.

SO, THAT'S ALL THAT'S LEFT OF IT?

THAT'S JUST DEBRIS FROM THE EXPLOSION. THE WRECK'S AT THE BOTTOM. FAR TOO DEEP TO EVER BE RETRIEVED.

ANOTHER HUNTING TROPHY FOR YOUR COLLECTION... A NICE RED STRIPE FOR YOUR JOLLY ROGER... ARE YOU PROUD OF THAT?

"THOSE WERE MY ORDERS. I JUST OBEY THEM. I DON'T DWELL ON THE WORLD OF TOMORROW.
"ALL I KNOW IS THAT TAKING DOWN THE U-864 WAS THE BEST WAY TO SHORTEN THIS WAR..."

CAPTAIN LAUNDERS, YOU'RE A HERO. YOU JUST MANAGED SOMETHING THAT NOBODY HAS EVER DONE BEFORE.
YOU ARE THE PRIDE OF HIS MAJESTY'S NAVY. FOR THAT, I SHALL RECOMMEND YOU AT ONCE FOR THE DISTINGUISHED SERVICE ORDER.
THAT'S... NOT NECESSARY... I MERELY DID MY DUTY.

YOU HAVE NO IDEA WHAT IT COST ME TO GET YOU OUT OF THAT HOLD, COLLINS.
YOU HAVE NO IDEA WHAT IT COST ME TO BE IN THERE THANKS TO YOU, GENERAL NEWTON.

ESPECIALLY FOR MERCURY...
SURELY YOU UNDERSTAND THAT THAT CARGO WAS SO VALUABLE, WE WANTED TO GET IT BACK INTACT AT ALL COSTS.
IN WHICH CASE, RELYING ON YOUR GREED WAS OUR BEST BET.
I ASSUME YOU'RE GOING TO HAVE ME COURT MARTIALED?
DESERTION, ATTEMPTED THEFT... YOU'RE DAMN RIGHT CAPTAIN DUKE COLLINS'LL BE COURT MARTIALED...
FOUND GUILTY, AND EXECUTED. BUT WHO CARES ABOUT HIM?
"COLLINS..." WERE YOU FOND OF THAT NAME?
NOT REALLY... I BARELY HAD TIME TO GET USED TO IT.
THIS WAR ISN'T OVER, CAPTAIN FITZGERALD. WE STILL WANT TO BE THE FIRST ONES TO BERLIN.
"ANOTHER BATTLE LOOMS...
"AND A MAN LIKE YOU WILL ALWAYS BE USEFUL TO US."
Berlin

A FRENCHMAN AND AN ITALIAN ON A U-BOAT

The question that drove Fabio and Massimo—the talented artist and colorist behind this book—and myself to bring this story to life is a common one: what would we have done if we had been born sixty years earlier? As the world and our respective hometowns became war zones and sank into fascism, what would have been our place and our roles in this conflict that marked the previous century?

From Paris and Rome, the many documentaries and photos we have collected give us images of a time that seems so close. It is true that the Second World War took place more than seventy-five years ago, but the people of that time drove cars, used electricity and telephones. They present a spectrum of images, each reminding us that it is, in fact, not so far away…even less so when fascist-inspired movements continue to gain traction in our current culture.

If we had lived through that period, Fabio, Massimo, and I would have been on opposite sides of the land. This irony reinforced our questioning of the choices we would have made. My maternal grandfather was a prisoner of war in Germany for almost four years, and the discovery of photos of him during the making of this book gave a powerful shock to my system. On the other side of the Alps, Fabio and Massimo's grandparents also lived through this dark period.

For many years, I had carried this story with me about the tracking of U-864—a fact of war discovered during research on a completely different subject. But inspiration often comes when you least expect it: you find what you are not looking for.

Of course, this story did exist, but the book you have just read is fiction. Commander Wolfram, James Launders, and his navigators Chalmers and Watson did exist, and this remains the only instance in which a submarine sank another while they were both underwater. That said, many of the characters in this book are imaginary or composite. Not that the official story was not romantic or interesting enough. In this regard, I am always reminded of Winston Churchill's famous quote, "At the highest level of Secret Service action, real facts have in many cases equaled, in all their aspects, the most fantastic inventions of adventure fiction and melodrama."

But the intimate and personal history of the sailors of U-864 is buried at the bottom of the North Sea, in the heart of the submarine's wreckage. There are no survivors to testify to what happened in this German submarine on a secret and perilous mission at a time when, for many, the war was coming to an end.

U-864 sailed from Kiel on December 5th, 1944. The Allies had landed in Normandy six months earlier and were moving inexorably toward Berlin. Paris had been liberated since the previous summer, and on the Eastern Front, the Soviets were advancing even faster toward the German capital.

The shadowy areas of this story seemed to us a wonderful way to explore this notion of commitment while confronting it with the fanaticism that had governed European history since the early 1930s.

We also wanted to highlight the sacrifice of millions of anonymous people and civilians. The active role of the Norwegian Resistance in tracking down U-864 was revealed many years later. It seemed important to us, even in a story that mixes great history with fiction, to pay tribute to these unknown heroes.

Would we have had the courage to resist against the occupying forces, to disobey the orders of our superiors, to continue to fight? These are questions that will continue to haunt me for the rest of my life. And even if the seeds of this war are echoed every day in our current events, from the economic crises to the rise of fascist ideas, I hope never to have to find an answer to them.

Mathieu Mariolle, September 2021.

* Winston S. Churchill, *Thoughts and Adventures*, 1932.

SKETCHBOOK

Early, unused character designs for Duke Collins.

Early character designs for Duke Collins.

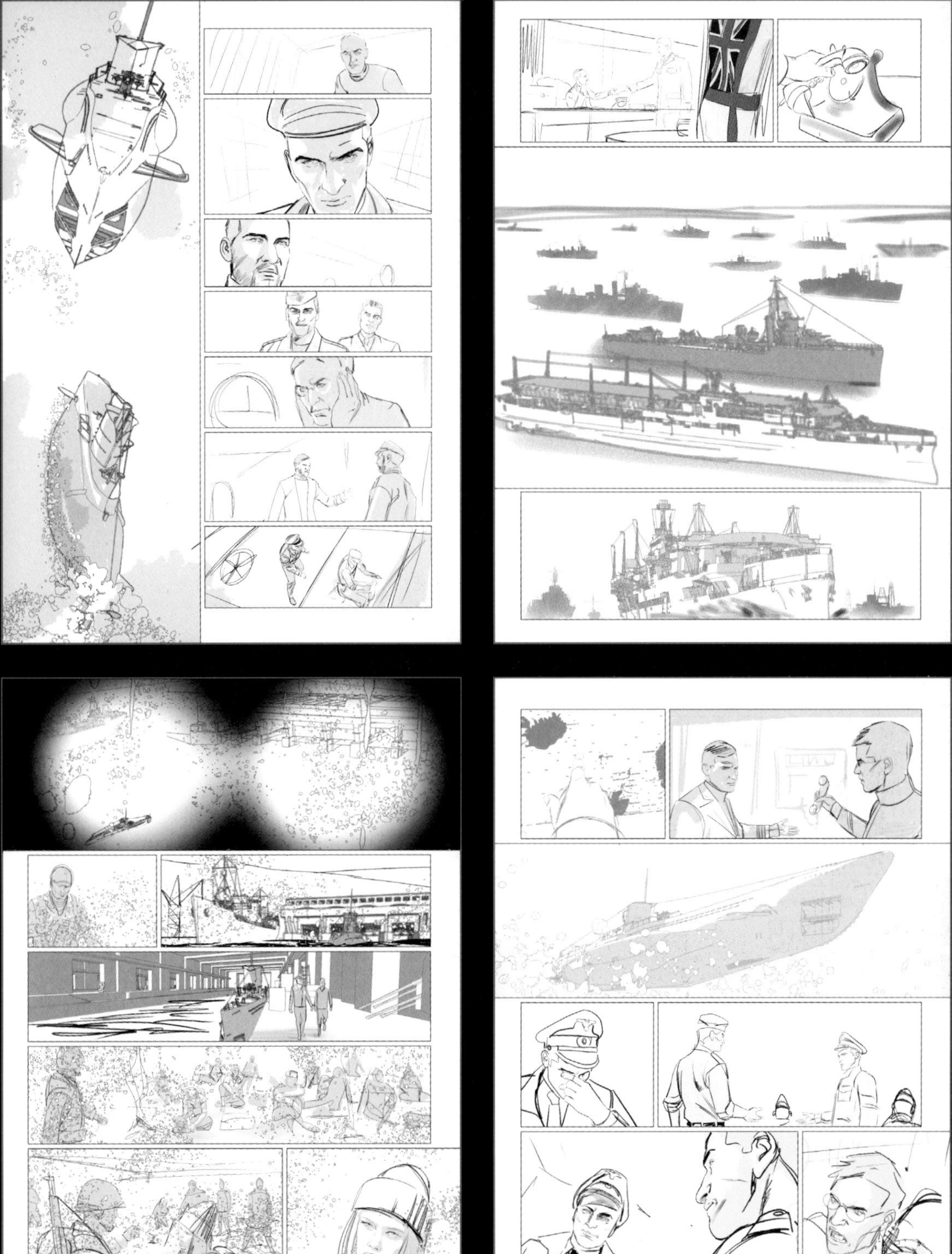

Storyboards and inks for pages 24, 31, 39 and 20 of *The Final Secret of Adolf Hitler*.

Inks for page 51 of *The Final Secret of Adolf Hitler*.

Inks for page 51 of *The Final Secret of Adolf Hitler*.

Unfinished cover illustration.